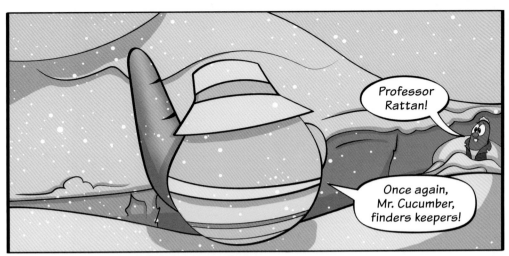

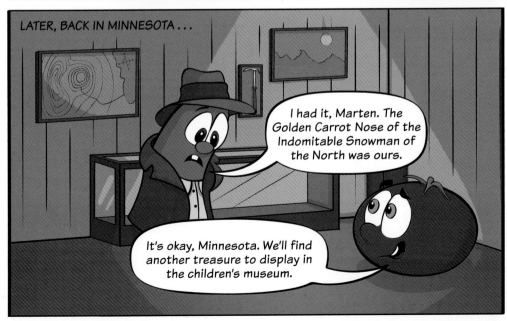

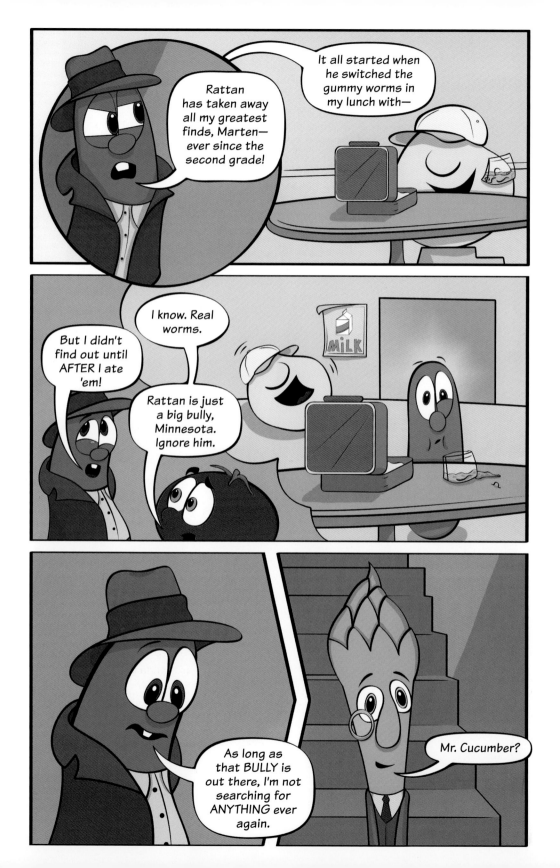

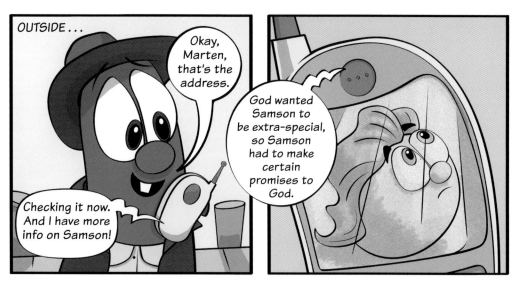

OUTSIDE . . .

Okay, Marten, that's the address.

Checking it now. And I have more info on Samson!

God wanted Samson to be extra-special, so Samson had to make certain promises to God.

He couldn't touch dead things, eat grapes, or cut his hair. But Samson didn't keep his promises, and—

Weird. But what about the address, Marten?

Hmm. That address isn't in Malta.

Rats! I'll check with Julia again.

INSIDE . . .

Great. First all the ice cream melts into a flood. Then the fan turns into a choppy-crushy thing. What's next?

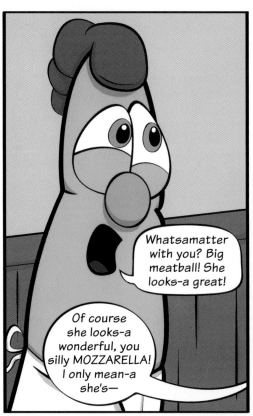

Whatsamatter with you? Big meatball! She looks-a great!

Of course she looks-a wonderful, you silly MOZZARELLA! I only mean-a she's—

Look, look fellas! We just came here to ask you something.

No problem, Bambina! Whatta you wanna know?

Gentlemen, we need to know about a hairbrush. Samson's Hairbrush.

Remove-a his cap!

Wait! I don't need a haircut!

And it's a FEDORA. Way cooler.

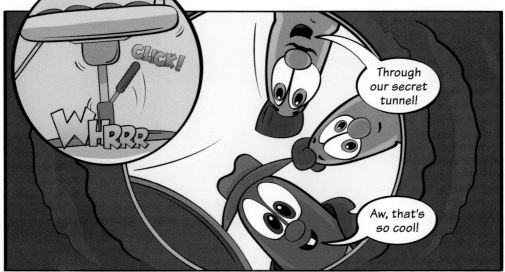

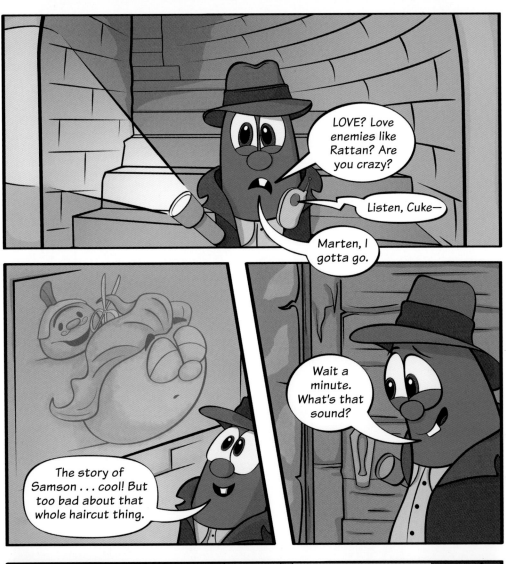

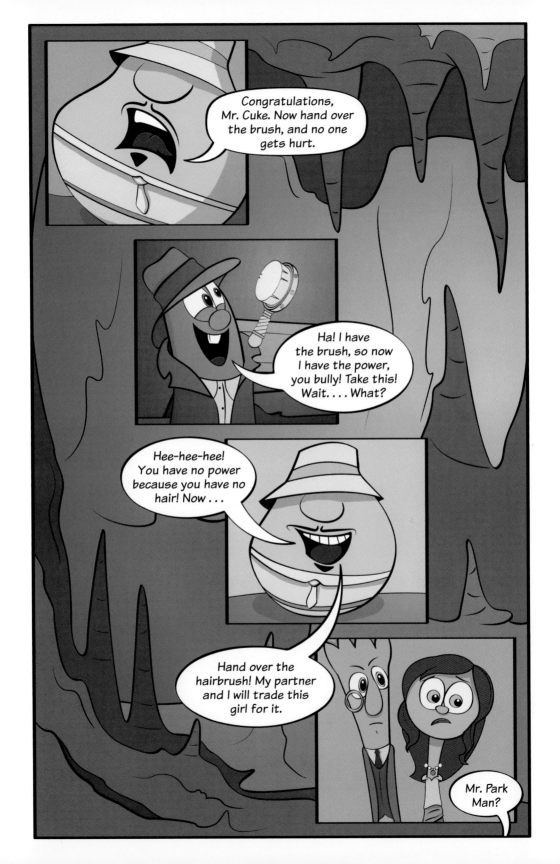

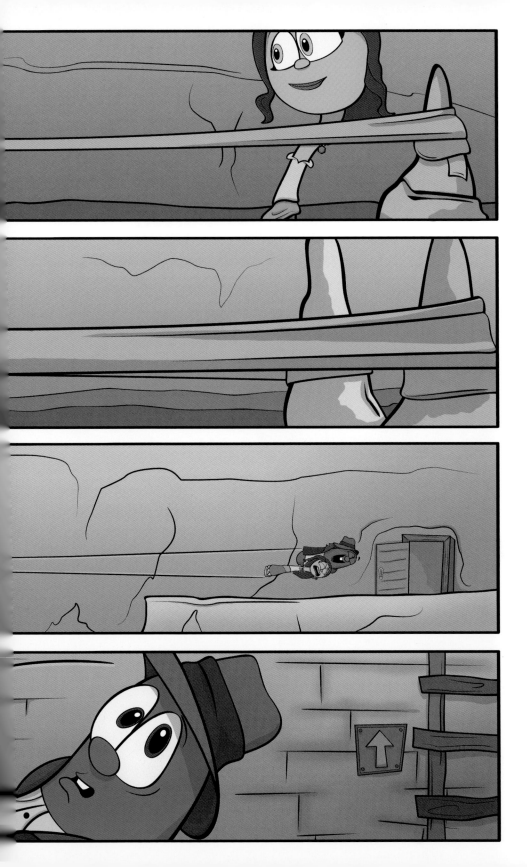

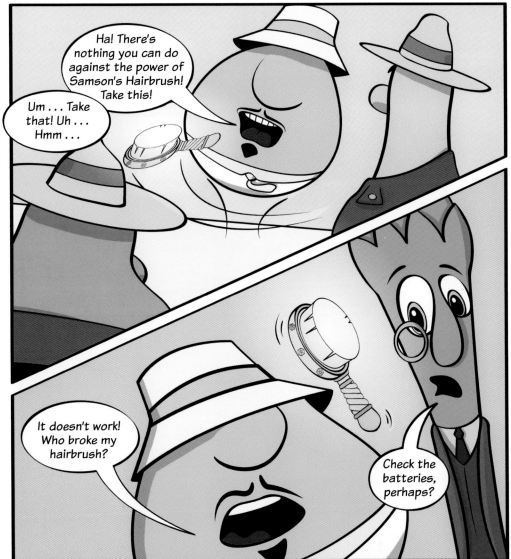

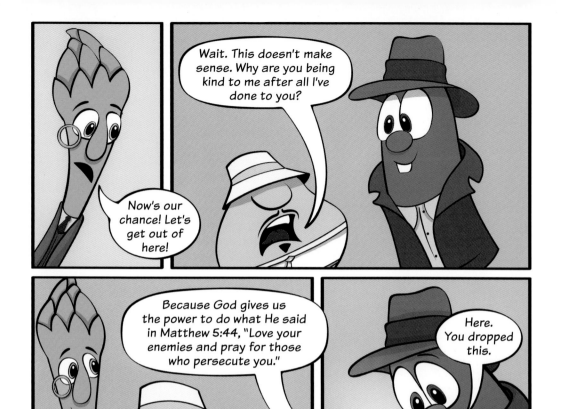